Collar Confusion

Nancy headed for Petra's backyard. George and Bess followed her.

Nancy glanced around. She didn't see Petra anywhere. But she did see Petra's dog, Prince Fabian. He was running around and around with a chew toy in his mouth.

Nancy's dog, Chocolate Chip, ran over to join him. The two dogs chased each other, barking happily.

"I wonder where Petra—" Nancy began. Then she stopped.

Nancy noticed that Prince Fabian was wearing a collar. A *jeweled* collar.

Prince Fabian was wearing Chip's missing collar!

The Nancy Drew Notebooks

# 1	The Slumber Party Secret	#25	Dare at the Fair
# 2	The Lost Locket	#26	The Lucky Horseshoes
# 3	The Secret Santa	#27	Trouble Takes the Cake
# 4	Bad Day for Ballet	#28	Thrill on the Hill
# 5	The Soccer Shoe Clue	#29	Lights! Camera! Clues!
# 6	The Ice Cream Scoop	#30	It's No Joke!
# 7	Trouble at Camp Treehouse	#31	The Fine-Feathered Mystery
# 8	The Best Detective	#32	The Black Velvet Mystery
# 9	The Thanksgiving Surprise	#33	The Gumdrop Ghost
#10	Not Nice on Ice	#34	Trash or Treasure?
#11	The Pen Pal Puzzle	#35	Third-Grade Reporter
#12	The Puppy Problem	#36	The Make-Believe Mystery
#13	The Wedding Gift Goof	#37	Dude Ranch Detective
#14	The Funny Face Fight	#38	Candy Is Dandy
#15	The Crazy Key Clue	#39	The Chinese New Year Mystery
#16	The Ski Slope Mystery	#40	Dinosaur Alert!
#17	Whose Pet Is Best?	#41	Flower Power
#18	The Stolen Unicorn	#42	Circus Act
#19	The Lemonade Raid	#43	The Walkie-Talkie Mystery
#20	Hannah's Secret	#44	The Purple Fingerprint
#21	Princess on Parade	#45	The Dashing Dog Mystery
#22	The Clue in the Glue	#46	The Snow Queen's Surprise
#23	Alien in the Classroom		
#24	The Hidden Treasures		

THE
NANCY DREW
NOTEBOOKS®

#45

The Dashing Dog Mystery

CAROLYN KEENE
ILLUSTRATED BY JAN NAIMO JONES

Aladdin Paperbacks
New York   London   Toronto   Sydney   Singapore

First Aladdin Paperbacks edition May 2002
First Minstrel Books edition December 2001

Copyright © 2001 by Simon & Schuster, Inc.

ALADDIN PAPERBACKS
An imprint of Simon & Schuster
Children's Publishing Division
1230 Avenue of the Americas
New York, NY 10020

The text of this book was set in Excelsior.

Printed in the United States of America
10 9 8 7 6 5 4 3

ISBN 0-7434-0693-1

1

A Holiday Party

"Guess what, Nancy? You got something in the mail!" Hannah Gruen announced.

Eight-year-old Nancy Drew glanced up from the book she was reading. Hannah, the Drews' housekeeper, was standing in the doorway of the living room.

Nancy smiled eagerly. "What is it, Hannah? What did I get?"

Hannah walked over to the couch where Nancy was sitting. She handed Nancy a bright pink envelope. "Maybe it's a Christmas card," Hannah said.

Nancy looked at the envelope. It was addressed to Miss Nancy Drew and Miss Chocolate Chip Drew.

Nancy peered over the edge of the couch. Her Labrador puppy, Chocolate Chip, was curled up on the floor, taking a nap. "Hey, Chip, this is addressed to you, too!"

Chip opened one eye and thumped her tail. Nancy reached into her pocket and pulled out a bone-shaped doggie biscuit. Chip got up on her hind legs and grabbed the biscuit with her teeth. She gobbled it up in about two seconds.

"Good girl!" Nancy said.

"Nancy, open the envelope. I'm dying to know what's in it," Hannah said with a chuckle.

"I will, I will."

Nancy opened the envelope carefully. Inside was a green card. It was shaped like a dog's paw.

The card said:

Dear Loyal Customer,
You are invited to a holiday party
to celebrate the grand reopening

of the Dashing Dog Pet Salon
this Friday, 2–5 P.M.
There will be lots of doggie treats
(and treats for humans, too!).
Hope to see you there!
Regards,
Rex Rumford
P.S.—At 4 P.M., we'll be raffling off a
beautiful, one-of-a-kind doggie collar
by Stella Sipowitz.
Don't miss it!

Chip began sniffing the invitation.

"Look, Chip! We're invited to a party at the Dashing Dog Pet Salon!" Nancy exclaimed.

Nancy had taken Chip to the Dashing Dog once. It was a fancy pet salon where dogs could get shampooed and trimmed and groomed. Chip had needed a professional bath because her fur had gotten covered with finger paint.

Hannah read the invitation over Nancy's shoulder. "A holiday party for dogs and their owners. What a great idea!"

"Do you think Dad will let Chip and me go?" Nancy asked Hannah. To Nancy, Hannah was way more than a housekeeper. Hannah had helped take care of Nancy since her mother had died five years ago.

"I'm sure he will. But let's ask him when he gets home from work, okay?" Hannah said. "In the meantime, who wants to help me bake some Christmas cookies?"

"I do!" Nancy raised her hand and jumped off the couch. Chip began barking. "I think Chip wants to help, too," Nancy said, laughing.

As Nancy followed Hannah to the kitchen, she clutched the paw-shaped invitation to her chest. She couldn't wait for Friday. If there was one thing she loved, it was a party!

"This place looks like a playland for dogs!" Bess Marvin said.

"They should call it Poochy Playland," her cousin George Fayne agreed.

Bess and George were Nancy's two best friends in the whole world. Nancy had invited them along to the Dashing Dog holiday party. Hannah had just dropped off the girls and Chip at the pet salon. She had promised to pick them up at 4:30.

The three girls stood inside the front door of the newly redecorated salon. Nancy remembered the way it had looked before, when she had brought Chip in for her bath. Back then, there was lots of pink furniture and pictures of glamorous dogs on the walls.

Now the salon had a whole new look. The walls were covered with wallpaper that had tiny pawprints on it. There were plush couches and chairs in red, blue, and yellow. In one corner was a big play area for dogs, with tunnels, balls, and other toys. A fluffy white poodle and a little brown terrier were playing tug-of-war with a rawhide bone.

In the far corner of the room was a doggie café called Bone Appétit. People sat on tall silver stools, sipping hot chocolate and eating cookies. Their dogs sat on low, wide stools and nibbled doggie biscuits. On the

CD player, a woman's voice sang "How Much Is That Doggie in the Window?"

In another corner of the room was an enormous Christmas tree. It was covered with sparkly lights and glittery ornaments shaped like dogs. A string of red bone-shaped holiday lights ran along the windows.

"Wow, this place is awesome!" Bess said. "I wish I had a dog. I'd come here all the time."

"So you could give your dog baths and stuff?" George asked her.

Bess shook her head. "No. So we could have snacks at Café Bone Appétit. Those cookies look yummy!"

Nancy giggled. Bess loved to talk about food almost as much as she loved to talk about clothes. George was a lot more into sports. The two of them were really different, even though they were cousins.

Chip tugged at her leash, eager to join the other dogs in the play area. "All right," Nancy said, unclipping the leash. "Be good, okay? No nipping or biting."

Chip bounded over to the play area. Nancy glanced around the room. It was crowded with two-legged and four-legged guests. Nancy spotted a girl from her school, Petra Wylie. Nancy wondered if Petra had a dog, too.

Nancy also saw Alice Cahill. She was the "Pet Corner" columnist for the *River Heights Gazette*. Nancy recognized Alice from her picture in the paper, since she and Hannah read "Pet Corner" every Tuesday.

Alice was petite and blond. She was talking to a couple of dog owners and scribbling in a small notepad. A big, fluffy white poodle was beside her, on a leash. Nancy wondered if that was Alice's pet, Pierre. Alice wrote about Pierre in her column from time to time.

"Welcome, welcome to the Dashing Dog!"

A man came walking up to Nancy and her friends. He was wearing a gray suit and a red bow tie. His eyes sparkled behind a pair of brown glasses.

"I'm Rex Rumford," the man said. He

smiled at Nancy. "You've been here before! I recognize you. Hmm, let's see. Chocolate Lab. Lots of paint. Emergency bath. Am I right?"

"Right!" Nancy laughed.

She introduced herself, and Bess and George did the same.

"Thank you for inviting me to your party," Nancy said. "I brought Bess and George with me. I hope that's okay."

"Oh, yes, the more the merrier," Rex said. He glanced at his watch. Its face had a picture of a cartoon dog on it. "Uh-oh, it's almost four o'clock. Excuse me, ladies. I need to make an announcement."

Rex went up to the front counter and rang a loud bell. Several dogs began barking. "Attention, please!" Rex shouted.

The barking dogs were shushed by their owners. The room fell silent.

"I have an announcement to make," Rex went on. "At four o'clock—"

But Rex didn't get a chance to finish. He was interrupted by a loud scream from the back of the room!

2

A Surprise Prize

W ho screamed?" Bess cried out. "What happened?"

Nancy whirled around. She saw a boy in the back of the room, inching away from a big Doberman. The Doberman was sniffing the boy's feet. All around the room, more dogs began to bark.

A middle-aged woman broke through the crowd and went rushing up to the boy. She was wearing a black dress with an expensive-looking diamond necklace. Nancy remembered seeing her the last time she was at the Dashing Dog. Her name was Mrs. Vanderpool.

"Come on," Nancy whispered to Bess and George. "Let's see what's going on." The three friends followed Mrs. Vanderpool.

Mrs. Vanderpool stopped in front of the boy and put her hands on her hips. "Lucas!" she exclaimed. "Why did you disturb Mr. Rumford's speech like that?"

"I'm sorry, Grandma," Lucas apologized. "But that mean dog tried to jump up on me." He pointed to the Doberman.

"Lucas, that is what dogs do," Mrs. Vanderpool said sharply. "They jump up on people. All you had to do was to tell the nice Doberman to get his paws off you and go play somewhere else. It's very simple."

"But, Grandma—" Lucas protested.

Just then two tiny Yorkies ran up to Mrs. Vanderpool. They were wearing matching red sweaters, and they had little red bows on their heads.

"My babies!" Mrs. Vanderpool cried out. She scooped them up and clasped them to her chest. "Hello, Muffy. Hello, Buffy. Aren't you the most precious babies in the world? Yes, you are! Does your mommy love you? Yes, she does!" The Yorkies began yipping and squirming in her arms.

"Is your grandson okay, Mrs. Vanderpool?" Rex called out.

"Yes, he's fine, thank you," Mrs. Vanderpool said, waving one hand. She frowned at Lucas and added, "I'm going to personally apologize to Mr. Rumford for your behavior." Then she turned and marched up to the front counter. The Yorkies were still yipping and squirming in her arms.

"Ankle biters," George muttered.

Nancy glanced at Lucas. He had blond hair and big brown eyes. He seemed to be the same age as Nancy and her friends.

"Hi, Lucas, I'm Nancy. And these are my friends Bess and George," Nancy said. "Hey, are you okay?"

Lucas stared down at the ground and kicked a doggie ball with his foot. "I guess so."

"That mean Doberman!" Bess said sympathetically. "I'd scream, too, if he jumped up on me."

Lucas smiled shyly. "I don't like dogs," he admitted. He stole a quick glance at his grandmother. She was across the room talking to Rex. "Don't tell *her* that, though," he added. "I like cats. I have two of them back home."

"Where do you live?" Nancy asked him.

"Chicago. I'm visiting Grandma for a week," Lucas replied.

Rex rang the loud bell again. "Ahem. Excuse me, everyone. Now, as I was saying. At four o'clock, which is in just ten minutes, we will be raffling off a beautiful jeweled doggie collar. It's made by local artist Stella Sipowitz. Here's Stella now, with the collar!"

A tall, dark-haired woman dressed in a red velvet cape joined Rex. She held up a red leather collar that was studded with rhinestones shaped like bones.

"This collar is part of a new line of special things for today's dashing dog," Stella announced. "More of my collars, coats, and

leashes are on sale here at the Dashing Dog Pet Salon. But this particular collar is one of a kind. So if *you're* the lucky raffle winner, your pooch will be the proud owner of a completely unique and original work of art!"

"Wow!" Nancy whispered excitedly to Bess and George. "That collar would look really great on Chip."

Rex raised his hands and clapped. "Thank you, Stella. Ladies and gentlemen, if you haven't already filled out your entry slips, please do so right now. The slips are right here on the counter. Fill out your name and phone number. Then put the slip in the jar. And remember—one slip per person, please. No exceptions!"

Everyone began rushing up to the front counter. "Did you fill out your entry slip yet?" Bess asked Nancy.

Nancy shook her head. "Not yet. Let's do that now."

Nancy, Bess, and George walked over to the front counter. Nancy filled out her entry slip with a black pen that was lying next to the raffle jar. When she was done, Bess took the pen from her. She started filling out an entry slip, too.

"But you don't have a dog, Bess," Nancy said, surprised.

Bess shrugged. "I know. But if I win, I could always give the collar to Chip as a Christmas present."

"Oh, that is so sweet!" Nancy exclaimed. "Chip would love that."

"I'll do that, too," George said. "Wouldn't it be cool if one of us won the collar for Chip?"

Hearing her name, Chip came bounding up to the girls. "Hi, Chip! Are you having fun?" Nancy asked her.

Chip jumped up on Nancy's leg and wagged her tail happily. "I think the answer is yes," Nancy said, giggling.

"Excuse me, are you done yet or what?"

Nancy turned around at the sound of the familiar voice. Petra Wylie was standing behind her. She looked annoyed.

"Other people need to fill out their entry slips, too," Petra snapped. She nodded at the black pen, which George was holding. "And there's only one pen."

"Oh, right. Sorry." George finished up her entry slip and put it in the raffle jar.

Nancy glanced down. Standing at Petra's feet was a small white dog with brown spots.

"Is that your dog, Petra?" Nancy asked her.

"Yes," Petra said.

Nancy reached her hand down to let the dog sniff it. "Wow, she's so cute. What kind is she?"

The dog growled at Nancy. Nancy quickly pulled her hand back.

"It's a *he*," Petra replied. "And he's a Jack Russell terrier. His name is Prince Fabian. I'm going to win the collar for him."

Bess crossed her arms over her chest. "No, I don't think so, because *we're* going to win the collar for Chocolate Chip!"

Nancy glanced at the raffle jar. "There are lots and lots of entry slips in there. Maybe *none* of us will win."

"We'll see!" Petra bent down and began

filling out an entry slip with big, loopy letters.

Chip bounded off in the direction of Café Bone Appétit. "I think Chip's trying to tell us something," Nancy said.

"I agree with Chip." Bess grinned. "It's snack time. Wait up, Chip!"

The three girls squeezed through the crowd. At the café they ordered muffins and hot chocolate for themselves. Nancy ordered a bowl of doggie treats for Chip.

As they ate, Nancy glanced across the room at the raffle jar. She saw that Mrs. Vanderpool was filling out an entry slip. The "Pet Corner" columnist, Alice Cahill, was standing next to her. She was filling out an entry slip, too.

Just as Nancy and her friends were finishing up their snacks, Rex rang the bell again.

"It's four o'clock, time for the raffle!" he announced. He reached into the jar and stirred the entry slips with his fingers. Then he covered his eyes with one hand and grabbed one of the slips.

Bess was bouncing up and down with excitement. "I have my fingers *double* crossed for good luck," she told Nancy and George.

"Mine are *triple* crossed," George said.

Slowly Rex removed the slip from the jar. He unfolded it. "And the winner is . . ."

Nancy, Bess, and George held their breath.

"Nancy Drew!" Rex announced. "Come on up here, Nancy!"

"Ohmigosh!" Nancy exclaimed.

Bess grabbed her hand and began jumping up and down. "You won, Nancy! You won!" she cried out.

Everyone in the room clapped. Dogs yipped and ran around in circles.

Nancy walked across the room to the front counter. Rex had set the collar on a black velvet cushion. Up close, it was even more beautiful. The bone-shaped rhinestones sparkled brightly against the red leather of the collar.

"Congratulations, Nancy," Rex said. "I hope your dog will enjoy this very special collar."

"Thank you," Nancy said, smiling. "She will."

Rex excused himself to welcome some guests who had just arrived. Just then Petra came marching up to Nancy. "I should have won that collar, and you know it!" she snapped. "It would look a lot better on Prince Fabian than on your . . . your . . . little brown mutt."

"That is a really mean thing to say," Nancy shot back.

"Humph!" Petra stuck her nose in the air and marched away. Prince Fabian followed obediently.

"Ignore her," George whispered to Nancy. "She's a spoiled brat."

Nancy nodded. "She sure is."

"Excuse me!"

Nancy turned around. Mrs. Vanderpool was standing there, smiling sweetly.

"Excuse me," Mrs. Vanderpool repeated in a low voice. "Nancy, is it? How much do you want for that collar? I *must* have it for one of my Yorkies."

Nancy was surprised by Mrs. Vanderpool's request. "Thank you, but it's not for sale," she said.

Mrs. Vanderpool stopped smiling. "Well!"

After she had gone, Bess said, "*Everyone* seems to want the collar."

"Yes, but it's Chip's," Nancy stated firmly. "We won it fair and square."

"That's right!" George agreed.

Nancy glanced at her watch. "Hannah will be picking us up in about twenty minutes," she said to her friends. "Let's check out the rest of the salon."

"Good idea," Bess said. George nodded.

Leaving Chip to play with a couple of other Labs, the girls began walking around the salon.

They saw the Shampooch Room. Rex was demonstrating his new line of bathing products on a really wet golden retriever.

They saw the Doggie Den, where a bunch of dogs were sitting on an overstuffed couch. They were watching cartoons about dogs chasing cats.

The Dashing Dog also had an outside

area. In it were a covered run, kennels, and a big patch of dirt. Petra's dog, Prince Fabian, was chasing a couple of other terriers up and down the run.

After a while the girls went back inside. The crowd had thinned somewhat. Nancy headed over to the counter so she could pick up the collar. Hannah would be arriving in just a few minutes.

Nancy got to the counter—and gasped. The black velvet cushion was there. But the collar was gone!

3

On the Case

Nancy glanced around the salon. The collar was nowhere to be seen.

Bess and George were standing nearby, checking out a display of doggie sweaters. "Bess! George!" she cried out.

"What's the matter?" George asked her.

Nancy pointed to the velvet cushion. "The collar is gone!" she announced.

"What!" Bess gasped.

Rex Rumford happened to pass by at that moment. His sleeves were rolled up, and his hands were still wet with shampoo and dog fur. "Hi, ladies. Are you enjoying your-selves?" he called out cheerfully.

"Mr. Rumford, have you seen my Stella Sipowitz collar?" Nancy asked him. "I left it here, and now it's gone."

Rex stopped in his tracks and frowned. "There must be some mistake."

"No, it's definitely gone," Nancy insisted.

"Hmm, well, maybe someone picked it up by mistake and set it down some-where," Rex said.

The four of them searched the area around the counter. There was no sign of the collar. Then they searched every inch of the salon. Chip trailed along, sniffing like a bloodhound.

But the four of them—plus Chip—had no luck finding the collar. It was definitely gone.

Nancy glanced around the salon, trying to figure out who might have seen the col-lar. But a lot of the guests had left, includ-ing Petra, Mrs. Vanderpool, and Lucas.

Alice Cahill stopped Nancy near the

doorway of the Doggie Lounge. Her green pen was poised over her notepad.

"Excuse me, but did I hear you say that your collar is missing?" she said eagerly. "I'm Alice Cahill. I write the 'Pet Corner' column for the *River Heights Gazette*. I'd *love* to have a quote from you for my column."

"A quote?" Nancy asked her.

Alice nodded. "Yes. As in, what do you think happened to your collar? Do you think there's a thief on the loose? Is River Heights being hit by a wave of doggie-collar crime? Do tell!" She glanced at her poodle, who was gnawing on a black leather backpack. "Pierre, you leave that nice backpack alone!"

Nancy thought for a moment. Could someone have stolen her collar? If so, who?

"I plan to get on the case," Nancy told Alice in a determined voice. "If there's a thief on the loose, I'm going to figure out who it is!"

"Nancy's a detective, Ms. Cahill," George piped up.

"Yeah, she's the best detective at Carl Sandburg Elementary School," Bess added. "She's solved lots and lots of mysteries."

Chip barked excitedly.

"Wonderful!" Alice said, scribbling like mad. "This is going to make a fabulous column!"

Nancy was happy that she was going to be in Ms. Cahill's "Pet Corner" column. But she would be a lot happier if she got her collar back—safe and sound!

That night at dinner Nancy told her father what had happened at the Dashing Dog Pet Salon. She had already filled Hannah in during the car ride home.

"You mean someone *stole* Chip's new collar?" Carson Drew said when Nancy had finished. "That's terrible!"

Nancy took a bite of her grilled fish. "I'm not *sure* if someone stole Chip's collar," Nancy murmured. "But it looks like it. And I'm going to find out who!"

"Do you have any suspects?" Hannah asked her.

Nancy mulled this over. "Hmm. Well, there's Petra Wylie. She goes to my school. She really, really wanted to win the collar for her dog, Prince Fabian. She kind of threw a fit when I won instead."

Carson broke off a piece of bread. "Sounds promising. Any other suspects?"

"There's also Mrs. Vanderpool," Nancy said after a minute. "She really wanted the collar, too—for one of her Yorkies. She has two of them, and their names are Muffy or Puffy or Buffy or something like that. Anyway, she actually offered to buy Chip's collar from me."

"Sounds like a prime suspect to me," Hannah remarked.

"I know you'll figure this out," Carson said. "You're the best detective I know, Pudding Pie." "Pudding Pie" was Carson's nickname for Nancy.

"Thanks, Daddy." Nancy grinned.

Later that night Nancy got out her special blue notebook. Her father had given it to her when she was trying to solve her first mystery. It helped her to keep track of suspects and clues.

She snuggled under the covers, picked up her pen, and began to write:

The Case of the Missing Doggie Collar
Suspects:
Petra Wylie, because she wanted the collar for her dog, Prince Fabian.
Mrs. Vanderpool, because she wanted the collar for one of her Yorkies.
Clues: ?????

Nancy reread what she had written. It gave her an idea. Tomorrow she would see if Bess and George could go with her to question the two suspects—in person.

Petra lived a few streets from Nancy. On Saturday morning Nancy got permission to walk over to her house. Bess and George got permission from their parents, too.

Outside, the air was brisk and cold. It felt as though it might start snowing any minute. As they walked, Nancy pulled her wool hat over her ears and rubbed her mittened hands together. Chip ran alongside her, keeping her nose low to the ground and sniffing every pebble and tree.

"I think Petra's totally guilty," George said.

"She was acting like a major spoiled brat yesterday," Bess agreed.

"I'm not sure. We'll have to find more clues before we can accuse Petra," Nancy said.

They soon got to Petra's house. It was big and pink, with green shutters and a huge wraparound porch. White holiday lights sparkled in all the windows, and a green wreath was hanging on the front door.

Nancy rang the bell. After a minute Mrs. Wylie answered. "Hi, girls, what can I do for you?" she asked pleasantly.

"Is Petra home?" Nancy said.

Mrs. Wylie smiled. "She's out back, playing with the dog. The easiest thing would be to go around the side and through the gate."

"Thank you," Nancy said.

Nancy headed for the backyard. George

and Bess followed her. Nancy's boots made squishing noises as she walked. The ground was muddy from when it had snowed and then thawed recently.

When they got to the backyard, Nancy glanced around. She didn't see Petra anywhere. But she did see Prince Fabian. He was running around and around with a chew toy in his mouth.

Chip ran over to join him. The two dogs chased each other, barking happily.

"I wonder where Petra is—" Nancy began. And then she stopped.

Then Nancy noticed that Prince Fabian was wearing a collar. A *jeweled* collar.

Prince Fabian was wearing Chip's missing collar!

4

Sniffing for Clues

Nancy couldn't believe her eyes. Prince Fabian was wearing the stolen collar!

"What are you doing here?"

Nancy turned around. Petra was walking out of the garage, carrying a big rubber ball.

Petra threw the rubber ball down on the ground. Both Prince Fabian and Chip dived after it.

Then Petra turned to Nancy with an angry expression. "I said, what are you doing here?" she repeated.

"I think the real question is, what is your dog doing with my dog's collar?" Nancy shot back.

"What?" Bess gasped. She glanced at Prince Fabian. "Nancy, you're right! Petra, *you're* the collar thief!" she said accusingly.

Petra looked surprised. "What? What are you two talking about? What collar thief?"

George put her hands on her hips. "You stole Chip's collar yesterday at the Dashing Dog!"

Petra's jaw dropped. "I did no such thing!"

Just then Prince Fabian came running in the girls' direction. "Come here, boy," Petra ordered. "That's right, over here. Heel!"

Prince Fabian skidded to a halt in front of Petra and wagged his tail expectantly. Petra pointed to the terrier's collar. "See? That is not Chip's collar," she said triumphantly. "It's *another* Stella Sipowitz collar. It's a lot prettier, if you ask me!"

Nancy bent down and took a closer look. Petra was right. Prince Fabian was not wearing Chip's collar.

Prince Fabian's collar was made out of stretchy red fabric, not leather. And the rhinestones were shaped like hearts, not bones.

"Um . . . I'm sorry I accused you," Nancy apologized. She explained to Petra that someone had taken Chip's collar the day before at the Dashing Dog.

When she had finished, she added, "Where did you get this collar, anyway?"

"At the Dashing Dog," Petra replied. "When my mom picked me up, I told her about not winning the raffle. So she came into the salon and bought me this collar instead."

Nancy apologized to Petra again. Then she, Bess, and George turned to leave.

Nancy had a hard time getting Chip to come with them. She was having such a good time playing with Prince Fabian. Nancy finally got her to part with her new friend after bribing her with a doggie biscuit.

"Now what?" Bess asked Nancy once they were out on the sidewalk.

"Now we go to my house to have lunch,"

Nancy said. "Then, afterward, we check out Suspect Number Two."

After a yummy lunch of grilled-cheese sandwiches and tomato soup, courtesy of Hannah, Nancy and her friends got permission to pay Mrs. Vanderpool a visit. Mrs. Vanderpool lived near the park where the girls liked to play.

This time Nancy left Chip with Hannah. It was Chip's nap time, anyway.

Mrs. Vanderpool's house was an enormous white mansion with big, tall columns. The girls walked down a path lined with low bushes and stone statues of Yorkshire terriers.

"Oh, brother," George said, rolling her eyes at the statues.

In a shady spot near the garage, Nancy thought she saw the melting remains of a snow statue. It looked suspiciously like a cat. She wondered if Lucas had made it.

Nancy knocked on the door. After a minute it was answered by a woman dressed in a maid's uniform.

"Yes, may I help you?" the woman said.

"We'd like to see Mrs. Vanderpool," Bess piped up.

"She's not home right now," the maid replied.

"How about Lucas?" Nancy said quickly.

The maid smiled and opened the door wider. "He's upstairs in his room. Why don't you go on up? It's the third door on the right."

Nancy grinned. "Thanks!"

Nancy, Bess, and George went through the doorway and up the marble staircase.

Mrs. Vanderpool's house was as fancy on the inside as it was on the outside. It was furnished with antique furniture and red velvet curtains. The walls were covered with gold-and-red wallpaper. There were several portraits of Yorkies in the front hallway.

"Why do you want to see Lucas?" Bess whispered to Nancy as they went up the stairs.

"If his grandmother took the collar, he might know something," Nancy whispered back. "Plus, this gives us an excuse to look for those Yorkies. Maybe one of them is wearing Chip's collar."

George gave Nancy a thumbs-up sign. "Good idea!"

When they got to the upstairs landing, Nancy turned and proceeded down the hall. She spotted the two Yorkies. They were crouched in front of a closed door and sniffing like mad.

"That's the third doorway on the right—Lucas's bedroom," Nancy whispered. "I wonder what's so interesting to those dogs?"

"Maybe Lucas is hiding a secret stash of doggie biscuits in his room," Bess suggested.

Nancy went up to the Yorkies. She saw that neither one of them was wearing Chip's collar. They were both wearing simple blue collars with dog tags on them.

"Oh, well," Nancy said with a sigh.

The Yorkies ignored her and continued sniffing. Nancy was surprised that they weren't yipping at her and her friends. The

Yorkies seemed a lot more interested in whatever was behind the closed door.

Nancy was about to knock on the door to see if Lucas was inside. Just then she heard footsteps behind her.

She turned around. Lucas was standing there. "You can't go in there!" he cried out.

5

Too Many Entries

Lucas ran past Nancy and flattened his body against his bedroom door. "If you go in there, you'll be in big trouble!" he warned.

Nancy frowned. Lucas seemed to be in a panic about something. What was going on?

Nancy pointed to the door. "That's your room, right?" she asked Lucas.

Lucas hesitated. "R-right. So?"

"So we were just looking for you," Nancy explained. "We wanted to ask you some questions and stuff."

Lucas glanced around nervously. "Questions . . . about what?"

"About your grandmother," George piped up.

"M-my grandmother?" Lucas repeated.

The Yorkies were still sniffing like mad at the closed door. One of them began yipping and scratching the wood on either side of Lucas. The other one joined in.

"By the way, what's in your room?" Bess asked Lucas. "More dogs? Or doggie biscuits? Or what?"

Lucas turned white as a ghost. "You all have to go!" he burst out. "Right now! I'm really, really super-busy, and besides, Grandma's going to be home any minute. Maybe we could do this question thing another time, okay?"

Nancy was going to argue with him, but he really wanted them to leave. "Come on, let's go," Nancy said to Bess and George. The three girls waved goodbye to Lucas and the yipping Yorkies and headed down the stairs.

Once they were back outside, George

turned to Nancy. "Why do you think Lucas was being so weird?"

"I don't know," Nancy said, pulling on her mittens. "He sure was acting suspicious."

"Nancy!" Bess gasped. "I just had an idea! What if *Lucas* is the collar thief?"

Nancy nodded. Bess's idea made sense. "That sure would explain why he wouldn't let us into his room. Maybe he was hiding Chip's collar in there."

She paused at one of the stone Yorkie statues. It had a bow around its neck. "On the other hand, Lucas doesn't even *like* dogs," she murmured. "So why would he steal the doggie collar?"

Carson Drew took a sip of coffee. "So how's your big case going, Pudding Pie?" he asked Nancy.

It was Sunday morning. The two of them were having brunch at Chez Meow, a restaurant in downtown River Heights. It was called Chez Meow because a cat named Meow lived there.

Nancy liked Chez Meow. There were

framed pictures of cats all over the bright yellow walls. Meow herself, who was big and white and fluffy, sat preening her fur in a sunny window.

While they ate, Nancy filled her father in on the day before. When she had finished, he said, "So you're adding Mrs. Vanderpool's grandson to the suspect list, eh, Pudding Pie?"

Nancy nodded. "Yes, Daddy. The problem is, I can't figure out a motive for him."

"Hmm, that *is* a problem," Carson agreed.

Nancy took a bite of her strawberry pancakes. Then she reached into her pocket and pulled out her special notebook.

She uncapped her pen and opened to the page about the missing-collar case. She wrote Lucas's name under "Suspects."

While Nancy wrote, Carson glanced at the Sunday paper. "Hey, look at this!" he said after a minute. "You're in the newspaper!"

Nancy's head whipped up. "What?"

Carson slid the newspaper across the table. He pointed to Alice Cahill's "Pet Corner" column. It said:

The Pet Corner
Special Sunday Bulletin
By Alice Cahill

We've all heard of white-collar crime. But doggie-collar crime? Friday, at the newly revamped Dashing Dog Pet Salon, owned by canine beauty wiz Rex Rumford, a Stella Sipowitz original disappeared under mysterious circumstances. After the collar was raffled off to third-grader Nancy Drew and her Lab, Mocha Chip . . .

"Mocha Chip!" Nancy cried out. "She got Chip's name wrong!"

"Keep reading," Carson said. "What else does she say?"

Nancy scanned the rest of the column. Alice mentioned how the collar had vanished while Nancy, Bess, and George walked around the pet salon. She also mentioned that Nancy planned to get on the case:

Says the amateur detective Drew:
"I'm going to conduct a dogged inves-
tigation and collar the collar thief!"

Nancy pointed to the quote. "I don't
remember saying that," she murmured.

Just then the front door of the restaurant
opened, and Alice Cahill breezed in. She
noticed Carson and Nancy sitting there.

She gave Nancy a little wave. "Hope you
enjoyed my column!" she called out. "Must
run! I'm here to interview Meow and her
owner for my *next* column!"

"Is that her?" Carson whispered to
Nancy.

Nancy nodded. "Uh-huh."

Alice sat down at a table and pulled out
her notebook and green pen. The owner of
Chez Meow scooped Meow up in her arms
and sat down across from Alice.

Nancy and Carson discussed the case
some more as they finished their brunch.
When they were done, Nancy asked her
father if they could stop by the Dashing
Dog before going home.

"I want to see if Rex Rumford found any new clues to the thief," Nancy explained.

"No problem, Pudding Pie," Carson replied.

A short while later they walked through the front door of the Dashing Dog. It was just around the corner from Chez Meow.

"Hello, hello," Rex greeted them. He was holding a small white collie in his arms. "I was just about to give Snowflake a special herbal bath. It's very relaxing. What can I do for you?"

"I'm still trying to find out who stole Chip's collar," Nancy told Rex. She hugged her blue notebook to her chest. "I'm trying to collect all the information I can."

Rex frowned. "I feel terrible about that. Just terrible! But I'm afraid I have no new information for you." He added, "What about you? Have *you* learned anything?"

Nancy was about to reply when she noticed something. The raffle jar from Friday was still on the front counter. She could see all the entry slips inside.

Most of the slips had black letters on them. She remembered that there had been a black pen sitting on the counter, for the guests to use.

But looking at the raffle jar now, Nancy saw that a bunch of entry slips had been filled out in a different color: green.

"That's strange," Nancy said out loud.

"What is it, Pudding Pie?" Carson asked her.

Nancy walked over to the jar and turned it upside down. The entry slips spilled out onto the counter.

Nancy picked out the slips with green ink on them. There were twelve of them. And the name on all of them was Cahill!

6

The
Thief Strikes Again

ancy couldn't believe it. Alice had stuffed the raffle jar with a dozen entry slips! She had wanted to increase her chances of winning the Stella Sipowitz collar.

Nancy turned to Rex. "Didn't you say on Friday that each customer got only one entry slip?" she asked him.

Rex nodded. "Absolutely! I was very clear about that."

Nancy's mind was racing. Alice must have wanted the Stella Sipowitz collar badly enough to break the rules.

Could she have wanted the collar badly enough to steal it? Nancy wondered.

"What's going on, Pudding Pie?" Carson asked her curiously.

"I need to talk to Alice Cahill right away," Nancy replied.

The two of them bid Rex goodbye and rushed back to Chez Meow. Alice was still there. She was wrapping up her interview with Meow and her owner.

"So what do you think is the best part of being a restaurant cat?" Alice asked Meow.

Meow purred loudly. Alice scribbled something in her notebook. "Uh-huh, I quite agree. Leftovers *are* a great thing! Well, that wraps up my interview."

Nancy waited until Meow and her owner had gotten up from Alice's table. Then she and Carson walked over to Alice.

Alice glanced up. "Oh, hello!"

"Excuse me, could I talk to you for a minute?" Nancy asked her.

"Uh-huh, sure," Alice said. "But then I *must* rush off. I have an interview with the mayor's pet parakeet in twenty minutes."

Nancy pulled from her pocket the dozen entry slips from the Dashing Dog. She let them tumble onto the table.

Alice gasped. "What . . . where did you . . ." Her eyes grew enormous.

"Rex Rumford said only one entry slip per customer," Nancy said. "There are *twelve* entry slips here."

"I . . . that is, well . . ." Alice fell silent.

Nancy stared at her and waited.

"Okay, I admit it," Alice finally confessed. "I wanted to make sure my precious Pierre won the collar. He would have looked so handsome in it!"

Nancy frowned. "Did you steal the collar after I won it, Ms. Cahill?"

Alice shook her head. "Absolutely not! I draw the line at stealing."

Nancy wasn't sure whether or not to believe her. Alice *seemed* to be telling the truth, though.

Alice glanced around the restaurant. "I beg you, don't tell anyone," she whispered.

"I'm not making any promises," Nancy

said. "If it turns out that you *did* steal Chip's collar . . . well . . ."

"I didn't," Alice insisted. "Dog's honor! I did *not* steal that Stella Sipowitz collar!"

"So we've got *four* suspects now," George said. "Petra, Mrs. Vanderpool, Lucas . . ."

" . . . and Alice Cahill," Bess finished.

As her friends talked, Nancy scribbled in her notebook. The three of them were sitting in Nancy's living room. After leaving Chez Meow, Nancy had invited them to her house to go over the latest developments in the case.

The girls were sitting around the coffee table. They were drinking hot cider and munching on popcorn. Carson Drew was in his study, catching up on some work. Nancy could hear him typing away on his computer.

Chip was curled up on the floor, taking a nap. She made soft snoring noises, and her body twitched from time to time.

"Petra's not such a strong suspect anymore," Nancy said as she scribbled. "Her mom bought Prince Fabian his own Stella Sipowitz collar."

"Yeah, but it's not as nice as yours," Bess pointed out.

Nancy nodded. "True." She took a sip of her hot cider, then added, "We still haven't talked to Mrs. Vanderpool. And as for Alice Cahill . . . she *said* she didn't steal Chip's collar. But she could have been lying."

Chip opened one eye and thumped her tail. She made a whimpering sound.

"Don't worry, Chip. We'll get your collar back," George reassured her.

Nancy reached into her pocket and pulled out a doggie biscuit. She handed it to Chip. Chip gobbled it down, then looked at Nancy expectantly.

"That's all I have, girl," Nancy told her. "Go back to sleep."

Bess scarfed down a handful of popcorn. "Personally, *I* think it's Lucas," she said. "He was acting totally guilty when we visited his grandma's house yesterday."

Just then the phone rang. "I'll get it, Dad!" Nancy called out.

She reached over to a side table and picked up the cordless extension. "Hello?"

"Nancy Drew?" The girl's voice on the other end sounded really upset.

Nancy frowned. "Who is this?"

"You know who it is. It's Petra Wylie."

Nancy glanced at Bess and George. "Oh, hi, Petra," she said. "What's up?"

"What's up? You know very well 'what's up,'" Petra cried out. "Prince Fabian's collar is gone. You stole it, Nancy Drew!"

7

A Yorkie Affair

Okay, tell us the whole story from the beginning," Nancy said to Petra. "When did Prince Fabian's collar disappear?"

Nancy, Bess, and George were sitting in Petra's living room. They had rushed over right after Petra had called.

Prince Fabian and Chip were playing in the backyard. Nancy could see them through the big picture window in the living room. They were digging a hole near the flowerbeds. Dirt was flying everywhere. Nancy hoped Petra's parents didn't mind.

Petra glared at Nancy. "I really don't know why we're having this conversation. Just admit it, Nancy. You stole Prince Fabian's collar!" she accused.

"Nancy is not a thief!" Bess said huffily.

George came to Nancy's defense, too. "Yeah, that's right!"

"Why would I steal Prince Fabian's collar?" Nancy asked Petra.

Petra shrugged. "I don't know. Because you're getting back at me for stealing Chip's collar, which I totally didn't do? Because you didn't want to buy a new collar? Whatever! I just want you to give back Prince Fabian's collar. Or I'm telling my mom!"

"Petra," Nancy said patiently. "I didn't steal Prince Fabian's collar. But I *will* help you find out who did. I need some information from you, though." She pulled her blue notebook out of her pocket and took the cap off her pen.

Petra looked suspicious. "Information?

What kind of information?" she demanded.

"Like, when was the last time you noticed Prince Fabian wearing his collar?" Nancy asked. She turned to a fresh page in her notebook.

Petra looked thoughtful. "Welllll . . . I guess that would have been at breakfast. I fed him a bowl of Doggie-O's and strawberries. He likes strawberries. I noticed that he was wearing the collar then."

"Uh-huh," Nancy said, scribbling. "And when did you notice that the collar was missing?"

"I guess about an hour ago," Petra replied.

"Were you and Prince Fabian here all morning?" George asked her.

Petra nodded. "Yup."

"How about guests or whatever? Did you have any friends over?" Bess piped up.

"That Mrs. Vanderpool lady came over to visit my mom and dad," Petra said. "She and my mom are on some committee or something. That weird kid was with her. Luke or whatever."

"Lucas," Nancy said slowly. She, Bess, and George exchanged a glance.

Nancy's mind began to race. Lucas had been at the Dashing Dog Pet Salon on Friday, when Chip's collar had disappeared. When Nancy and her friends were at his grandmother's house, he had acted really strange. And today Petra said that he was at *her* house—right before Prince Fabian's collar disappeared.

It was obvious. Lucas must be the collar thief!

Nancy jumped to her feet. "Come on," she said to Bess and George.

"What?" George said. "Where are we going?"

"To catch our collar thief," Nancy said excitedly.

When Nancy, Bess, and George arrived at Mrs. Vanderpool's house, there was a long row of cars parked in the driveway. The stone Yorkie statues along the front path were lit up with sparkly white holiday lights.

"I wonder what's going on?" Nancy said.

When the girls knocked on the door, the maid answered. "I'm afraid Mrs. Vanderpool is entertaining," she apologized.

Five Yorkies came running up to the door. They jumped up on the maid and made yipping noises. "Stop that! Down!" she ordered them.

"Did Mrs. Vanderpool get a bunch of new ankle biters . . . I mean, Yorkies?" George asked her.

The maid shook her head. "No. The members of her kennel club are here. They all own Yorkies."

"Myra, who's there?"

Mrs. Vanderpool came to the front door. She was wearing a red-and-green holiday sweater with a Yorkie design on it. "Come in, come in," she greeted the girls. "Did you change your mind about selling me that lovely Stella Sipowitz collar?" she asked Nancy.

Nancy was surprised. Mrs. Vanderpool must not know that the collar is missing, she thought.

Out loud, she said, "We're here to visit Lucas."

"Oh, how wonderful!" Mrs. Vanderpool exclaimed. "I think he's up in his room."

Nancy tied Chip's leash to the stair railing and promised to come right back. Then the girls followed the maid and Mrs. Vanderpool into the house.

There were Yorkies running around everywhere, yipping at each other. Nancy could see at least ten people in the living room. They were standing around and drinking coffee. They didn't seem to notice all the noise that the Yorkies were making.

"Third door on the right," Mrs. Vanderpool said, nodding at the stairs. "I'm sure Lucas will be glad to see you."

She excused herself and went back to her guests. Nancy and her friends started to go upstairs.

Then Nancy caught sight of Lucas. He was walking down the hallway, away from the living room and all the guests. He kept slipping his hand in and out of his shirt pocket. He didn't seem to notice Nancy and her friends.

"There he is!" Nancy whispered to Bess and George. "Let's follow him!"

"Where do you think he's going?" Bess whispered back.

"I don't know," Nancy replied. "But he seems to have something in his pocket."

"Maybe it's the collar," George whispered.

"Or the collars, *plural!*" Bess corrected her.

The three girls followed Lucas down the hallway. They tried to walk as quietly as possible. Every few seconds they ducked behind a piece of furniture so Lucas wouldn't spot them.

Lucas soon reached a door at the end of the hallway. He opened it and started down a set of stairs.

"He's going down to the basement," Nancy whispered.

They followed him down the stairs on tiptoes. The light in the basement was dim.

At the bottom Lucas stopped and reached into his shirt pocket. He began to pull something out. . . .

"Stop! Hand over the stolen loot!" Nancy cried out.

8

Unburied Treasure

Lucas whirled around. His hands fell to his sides. His eyes flashed with fear.

"I said, hand over the stolen loot!" Nancy repeated.

"S-stolen loot?" Lucas stammered. "W-what stolen loot?"

"The doggie collars," Bess said. "Chip's collar and Prince Fabian's collar. You stole them!"

Lucas glanced around frantically. "What are you talking about? I didn't steal any collars," he insisted.

Nancy pointed to his bulging shirt pocket. "What's in there, then?"

Lucas gulped. He reached into his pocket and pulled out something shiny.

Shiny and round.

It was a can!

Nancy peered at it closely. There was a label on it. "Kitty Deelight Gourmet," she read. "Huh?" She was totally confused.

Just then Nancy heard a tiny meowing sound. A scruffy yellow kitten came bounding out from behind some cardboard boxes. It purred and rubbed up against Lucas's leg.

"Hey, it's a kitty!" George exclaimed.

"Her name is Sunshine," Lucas said. He bent down to pet her. "I mean, that's what I named her, anyway."

"Is she yours?" Nancy asked him curiously.

"I found her wandering around in the park yesterday morning," Lucas explained. "She's a stray. I brought her home so I could clean her up and give her some food."

"Oh, that is so sweet!" Bess gushed.

"How do you know she's a stray?" George asked him.

"She was really, really dirty when I found her. I don't think anyone's been taking care of her," Lucas replied.

"Oh," George said. "Poor thing!"

Nancy had a sudden thought. "Is *that* what you were hiding in your room yesterday?" she asked Lucas. "Is that why the Yorkies were going crazy and sniffing your door?"

Lucas nodded. "I was hiding Sunshine in my room. But the Yorkies were getting way too curious. So I decided to bring her down here. The Yorkies hate the basement."

"So your grandmother doesn't know about Sunshine?" George said.

Lucas's eyes grew huge. "No way! She'd be so mad! Please don't tell her, okay? I'm going to keep Sunshine down here till next week. Then I'll take her home with me."

Nancy grinned. "Your secret's safe with us."

*   *   *

"Lucas isn't the collar thief," Nancy announced to Petra.

Nancy, Bess, and George had stopped by Petra's house on their way home. They wanted to tell her the news in person.

"Then who stole Prince Fabian's collar?" Petra whined. "My mom's going to be really mad when she finds out I lost it."

"Don't worry, we'll find it," Nancy reassured her. "But for the moment, we're back to square one."

Nancy pulled her blue notebook out of her pocket. She was about to open it when she heard a scratching noise at the back door. Petra got up to open it.

Prince Fabian ran through the door. His claws clicked against the hardwood floor. He had something in his mouth. Chip was right behind him.

"What is it, boy? What have you got?" Petra asked Prince Fabian.

Prince Fabian dropped something at Nancy's feet. It was his collar!

"Ohmigosh," Bess said. "Prince Fabian found his collar!"

"Where did you find it, boy?" Petra asked him.

Nancy picked up the collar. It was crusted with dirt.

Then it came to her.

"I know where Chip's collar is!" Nancy announced with a smile.

George stared at her. "Where?"

"The Dashing Dog Pet Salon," Nancy replied.

"Okay, Prince Fabian, lead the way," Nancy ordered him.

She, Bess, George, and Petra were at the Dashing Dog. Mrs. Wylie had driven them there. Rex Rumford was there, too. He had just finished grooming a couple of Dobermans.

"What is going on, may I ask?" Rex asked Nancy as he dried his hands on a towel.

"We're about to solve a mystery," Nancy explained.

She opened the back door of the pet salon. Prince Fabian bounded out, followed by Chip.

"Go ahead, boy! Find the collar!" Nancy called out to Prince Fabian.

"I still don't understand any of this," Petra complained. "What does *my* dog have to do with *your* dog's missing collar?"

Prince Fabian ran to the big patch of dirt near the covered run. He began digging like mad. He pulled out a red rubber ball, a chew toy, and a rawhide bone. Chip sniffed at each toy that Prince Fabian unearthed.

Then Prince Fabian pulled out a red leather collar. The collar had bone-shaped rhinestones on it.

"Prince Fabian, you found the collar!" Petra gasped.

Nancy took the collar out of Prince Fabian's mouth and rubbed the dirt off with her hands. Soon it was as good as new.

"I don't get it," George said to Nancy. "How did you know Chip's collar was here?"

"I figured it out when I saw Prince Fabian's collar with dirt all over it," Nancy explained. "Prince Fabian must have gotten hold of Chip's collar at the party. Then he buried it back here."

"That is brilliant! Simply brilliant!" Rex cried out. "I must call Stella Sipowitz right away to tell her the good news!"

Nancy put the collar around Chip's neck. The rhinestones glittered brightly against her dark brown fur. "There. You look beautiful," Nancy told Chip. Chip barked happily.

Two days later Nancy read Alice Cahill's "Pet Corner" column over breakfast:

The latest in the mystery of the missing doggie collar! Nancy Drew busted the case wide open on Sunday afternoon, when she discovered that the culprit was none other than a Jack Russell terrier named Prince Fabian. Way to go, Nancy!

Chip made a whimpering noise. She was sitting under the table. Nancy slipped her a piece of her bagel. Chip wolfed it down and wagged her tail.

The jeweled collar looked really pretty on Chip. Nancy was really glad that she had found it.

Nancy pushed the newspaper aside. Then she opened her blue notebook, picked up her pen, and began to write:

Sometimes it turns out that a crime isn't a crime at all. I thought a thief stole Chip's collar. But it turned out that it wasn't a thief. It was just a dog acting like a dog!

Case closed.

EASY TO READ—FUN TO SOLVE!

**Meet up with suspense and mystery
in The Hardy Boys® are:**

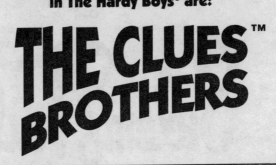

THE CLUES™ BROTHERS

#1 The Gross Ghost Mystery

#2 The Karate Clue

#3 First Day, Worst Day

#4 Jump Shot Detectives

#5 Dinosaur Disaster

#6 Who Took the Book?

#7 The Abracadabra Case

#8 The Doggone Detectives

#9 The Pumped-Up
Pizza Problem

#10 The Walking Snowman

#11 The Monster in the Lake

#12 King for a Day

#13 Pirates Ahoy!

#14 All Eyes on First Prize

#15 Slip, Slide, and Slap Shot

#16 The Fish-Faced
Mask of Mystery

#17 The Bike Race Ruckus

2389